go ahead,

ASK ME.

ALSO BY NICO MEDINA

The Straight Road to Kylie
Fat Hoochie Prom Queen

go ahead, ASK ME.

By Rico Medina + Billy Merrell

SIMON PULSE
NEW YORK LONDON TORONTO SYDNEY

SIMON PULSE
An imprint of Simon & Schuster Children's Publishing Division
1230 Avenue of the Americas, New York, NY 10020
First Simon Pulse paperback edition October 2009

For information about special discounts for bulk purchases, please contact Simon & Schuster Special Sales at 1-866-506-1949 or business@simonandschuster.com.
The Simon & Schuster Speakers Bureau can bring authors to your live event. For more information or to book an event contact the Simon & Schuster Speakers Bureau at 1-866-248-3049 or visit our website at www.simonspeakers.com.
Designed by Cara E. Petrus
The text of this book was set in Blockhead.
Manufactured in the United States of America
10 9 8 7 6 5 4 3 2 1
Library of Congress Control Number 2008944013
ISBN 978-1-4169-8692-8
ISBN 978-1-4169-9691-0 (eBook)

For Dan Poblocki, who might have seen a ghost.
Seriously.
And for Christina LaPrease, backwoods back in style.
Choctaw!

ACKNOWLEDGMENTS

Thanks to Jen Klonsky and the Pulse team,
especially Emilia Rhodes.

—N + B

INTRODUCTION

Go ahead, ask us how this book works. We'll tell you. . . . It's simple, really. Get a group of friends, pour yourselves some drinks, pop some popcorn, nuke some nachos, roast a pig—whatever floats your boat—then gather round and get comfortable. Now, open the book . . . and prepare to get **un**comfortable!

Seriously, though, some of these questions will make you cringe. But some will make you laugh, while others might make you stop and think. These questions are designed for Maximum Fun

Potential—a sort of party game, if you will—but if it ain't fun for you to divulge **everything** about yourself, you don't have to answer anything you're not comfortable with. However, passing comes at a price. . . .

IF YOU SKIP ON ANSWERING A QUESTION, YOU MAY:

A. Give someone in the room a compliment.

B. Make a critical comment about yourself.

C. Do an animal impression of your friends' choosing.

D. ______________________

(You and your friends pick.)

Now, go forth and be revealing! Honest! Lighthearted! Awkward! . . . And don't forget: the fun is in all those dirty little details. We hope you have as good a time reading and answering these questions as we had writing them.

Nico and Billy
Brooklyn, NY
January 2009

go ahead, ASK ME.

By Rico Medina + Billy Merrell

1. You're at your sex-god/rock-idol's concert with all your besties, and when the lights come on after the last encore, a roadie approaches you. You're invited backstage, but there's a catch: your . . . **FRUMPIER** friends ain't invited. Do you ditch your friends and hang with the band?

2. HOT OR NOT: TACO BELL.

3. If you could be made into an expert in one thing, what would that one thing be?

4. How do you want to spend your twilight years?

5. AGREE OR DISAGREE: CATS CAN READ YOUR THOUGHTS, AND THEY DON'T GIVE A SHIT.

6. Your best girlfriend is growing a seriously Frida Kahlo-esque 'stache. What do you do? What if, in the summer, the bikini line becomes the problem . . . ?

7. What's the **NASTIEST** thing a friend could leave in your bathroom to push you over the edge to say something to them, even though it'd be vomit-inducingly awkward? Oh. And what's the grossest thing someone could "drop off" that would make you never want to hang out with them ever again? **EVER** again.

8. WHO WOULD YOU RATHER HAVE PUNCH YOU IN THE FACE—A PRIEST, A NUN, OR A RABBI?

9. Who would you rather have as a college dorm-mate: an all-night-long gamer, an aspiring saxophonist, or an OCD clean-freak?

10. Who would you rather face in a fight—aliens or zombies?

11. Favorite body part?

12. AGREE OR DISAGREE: I LIKE TO HURT PEOPLE.

13. What's the worst part about getting old?

14. Is there a difference between tacky and tasteless?

15. Lab-partner arrangements are in . . . and you're placed with your arch-nemesis, your bitterest enemy. The one person in school who you wouldn't mind seeing flattened by a bus. What do you do? Are you thinking **SABOTAGE** . . . or **ABANDON SHIP**?!

16. WHICH IS WORSE FOR THE ENVIRONMENT: NOT EVER RECYCLING OR RAISING FIVE KIDS TO ADULTHOOD?

17. If you opened a themed restaurant, what would the theme be? What would the specialty of the house be?

18. Hot or not: iPhones.

19. Vampires or werewolves—which are scarier?

20. How, and at what age, would you explain to your kid about their gay aunt or uncle?

21. TRUE OR FALSE: I PEE IN THE SHOWER.

22. What was the best concert you've ever been to? If you haven't been to one, who do you want to see the most, and why?

23. Truth or Dare, or a nice game of cards?

24. WOULD YOU DATE SOMEONE WHO WAS MISSING TWO FINGERS?

25. Which is most essential, a bigger-screen TV or a better sound system?

26. Do you have an e-mail account no one but you knows about?

27. Favorite war?

28. FUN OR DANGEROUS: SWIMMING WITH DOLPHINS.

29. What is your absolute **BIGGEST** pet peeve?

30. What's the most hurtful thing anyone has ever done to you? What's the most hurtful thing you've done to someone else?

31. AGREE OR DISAGREE: RACISM IS STILL RAMPANT IN AMERICA.

32. Girls who have a lot of sex are typically labeled as whores, sluts, ho-bags, what-have-yous . . . and guys who'll stick it in anything that moves are thought of as players. Do you agree with this statement? Do you think it's fair?

33. Freckles: love 'em or hate 'em?

34. HOW AND WHEN DID YOU GET YOUR BIRDS-AND-THE-BEES TALK?

35. DEATHMATCH: HARRY POTTER VERSUS EDWARD CULLEN—WHO WINS?

36. Would you rather be locked in solitary confinement for a year or trapped alone on a desert island for a year?

37. How do you explain the process of photosynthesis to your beyond-doable lab partner in the sexiest way you know how? If you couldn't give two craps about photo-what's-her-face, just make something up.

38. AGREE OR DISAGREE: I AM LUCKY.

39. Have you ever gone commando? (The beach doesn't count.)

40. HAVE YOU EVER HAD TO FRIENDSHIP-DUMP SOMEONE? EVER WANTED TO?

41. Would you (or do you) fondle a crowd-surfer at a concert as they passed overhead?

42. You get to publicly shame someone— who is it, and how do you do it?

43. Which teacher gets the least respect at your school? Does he or she deserve it?

44. GOOGLE IMAGE SEARCH "DENTAL DAM." ANY THOUGHTS?

45. Fun or dangerous: Spin the Bottle.

46. Would you rather travel by plane, train, or automobile?

47. DESCRIBE YOUR DREAM HOME.

48. Agree or disagree: J-Lo should just give it up.

49. What's your opinion on the people who set up camp outside Wal-Marts the day after Thanksgiving?

50. Do you search through people's medicine cabinets? Purses or wallets? Underwear drawers? Bedside tables?

51. WHAT'S THE WORST WAY TO DIE?

52. Death match: A wasted Amy Winehouse versus a sharp corner? Place your bets.

53. Have you ever masturbated in your sleep?

54. WHEN WAS THE LAST TIME YOU CRIED, AND WHY (IF IT'S NOT TOO PERSONAL)?

55. Agree or disagree: To get ahead in life, you have to be a little bit mean.

56. Your most annoying friend can get you a job . . . but you have to work with him or her **CONSTANTLY**—what do you do?

57. TYRA OR OPRAH?

58. You're in line for a concert or to get into a club, and this homeless guy carrying a lobster won't go away, and is **TOTALLY** harassing you and your friends for money. How do you deal with the situation?

59. At a sleepover, one of your friend's parents offers to get you stoned. To toke or not to toke? Does it make a difference if it's your friend's mom or dad? Or if it's weed or whiskey? What about Xanax or Valium?

60. WHAT ANNUAL EVENT STRESSES YOU OUT THE MOST?

61. What do you consider to be the most erotic musical instrument?

62. Hot or not: Martha Stewart in her prison jumpsuit.

63. What's the scariest restaurant in your hometown after midnight?

64. If you could choose your parents, who would they be?

65. AGREE OR DISAGREE: PEOPLE CAN CHANGE.

66. Describe your ideal life in the Witness Protection Program.

67. IF YOU WERE TO BE EXECUTED, WHAT WOULD YOU PICK AS YOUR LAST MEAL?

68. Are other people's political views important to you? Could you be friends or lovers with someone whose views are at complete odds with yours?

69. What **ARE** your views on some of these hotly debated issues: abortion, gay rights, capital punishment, welfare? Any others you wanna talk about?

70. Death match: A Beta fish versus drowning angry fire ants—who wins?

71. What is your most unreasonable phobia?

72. What's worse to find in your hotel room: pubic hair on the bed or piddle stains on the toilet seat (and maybe a little on the floor surrounding the toilet)?

73. Agree or disagree: It is okay to defecate in natural bodies of water.

74. IS IT WORSE TO HAVE BAD SKIN OR BAD TEETH?

75. Camping or hotels?

76. WOULD YOU EVER SEND NAKED PICTURES OF YOURSELF TO YOUR SIGNIFICANT OTHER?

77. You and your friend get wasted at a party and pass out together. You wet the bed. Do you roll over and blame your friend or try to find a way to clean it up?

78. Who would you rather fool around with, a hot cousin or a hot step-sibling?

79. Do you want to get married? If so, why? When?

80. HOT OR NOT: STEAK.

81. What's the hottest foreign accent? The hottest regional American accent?

82. When you hear the words "laugh bomb," what do you think?

83. Agree or disagree: We all look the same in the dark.

84. HAMBURGER HELPER OR CHEF BOYARDEE?

85. If you were a prostitute, what would you charge for your various sexual services? Would you have a specialty?

86. Have you ever forced yourself to vomit?

87. WHICH BOOK WOULD YOU MOST LIKE TO BURN?

88. Agree or disagree: Goatees are for jackasses.

89. Who's hotter—cops or firefighters?

90. IF YOU COULD PICK ONE SUPERPOWER TO POSSESS, WHAT WOULD IT BE?

91. Would you ever pick up a hitchhiker? What if it's just some harmless-looking kid caught in an end-of-the-world thunderstorm?

92. What is the most memorable choreographed dance scene or video?

93. WHO IS THE CRAZIEST, LOCK-THAT-CRAY-CRAY-UP CELEBRITY?

94. Your best friend's significant other hits on you—and not in a cute in-front-of-your-best-friend sort of way. What to do? Bitch-slap? Flirt back? Play it cool, then fill your friend in?

95. HOT OR NOT: SCARVES.

96. What's the most impressive dish you know how to cook?

97. Have you ever Googled "Harry Potter's penis"?

98. AGREE OR DISAGREE: DUDES WHO SING AND PLAY GUITAR IN PUBLIC PLACES ARE DOUCHEY.

99. Are you at all superstitious? Do you have any good-luck charms?

100. WOULD YOU RATHER BE A LUNCH LADY OR A JANITOR?

101. Would you steal if you knew you wouldn't get caught?

102. In your not-so-humble opinion, what is the hands-down best music video ever created?

103. You're at a crowded beach with your best friend and the person you're dating. You get stung by a jellyfish, and all of a sudden your foot starts to feel like it's being stabbed by needles. You've heard that urinating on the affected area makes the stinging go away, but you just peed in the ocean! Who would you rather have shower you in gold? Your best friend? Or your significant other?

104. FAVORITE PIZZA TOPPING?

105. Agree or disagree: Truth is relative.

106. Which is the scariest cartoon character?

107. HAVE YOU EVER TASTED YOUR OWN BLOOD, AND IF SO, DID YOU LIKE IT?

108. Agree or disagree: Al Pacino plays essentially the same character in every movie he stars in.

109. What songs on your iPod do you try to keep a secret?

110. WOULD YOU RATHER BE RAISED BY WOLVES, LIONS, OR ALCOHOLICS?

111. Hot or not: Demi Moore.

112. NAME FIVE OBJECTS YOU COULD NOT LIVE WITHOUT.

113. What would the title of your autobiography be?

114. Agree or disagree: I would make a good game-show host.

115. WHAT'S THE WORLD'S MOST OVER-RATED LANDMARK?

116. If you had to do a striptease in front of one of your best friends, who would it be? And what object nearest you would you use as a prop?

117. You've thrown caution to the wind and find yourself having sex with your significant other in your bedroom with the door unlocked. Who would you rather have accidentally walk in on you doin' the nasty: your parents, your grandparents, or your little sibling?

118. WOULD YOU RATHER BE ADDICTED TO GAMBLING OR ROBITUSSIN?

119. If you were to die now and become reincarnated as some famous person's child—living or dead—whose child would you want to be? Whose would you **LEAST** want to be?

120. A teacher who you really trust asks if you can help him score some good weed. Would you?

121. FUN OR DANGEROUS: USING FOOD DURING SEX.

122. Would you rather have no eyebrows or no eyelashes?

123. Would you spend the night in a haunted house?

124. AGREE OR DISAGREE: POKING SOMEONE ON FACEBOOK IS ULTIMATELY UNSATISFYING.

125. Are history books objective?

126. Would you rather sell insurance or hearing aids?

127. Death match: Transformers versus The Incredible Hulk. Your prediction?

128. You're in your girl- or boyfriend's bathroom, and you've realized—too late!—that there are only about four squares of toilet paper left. What do you do?

129. WHAT'S HOTTER: MONEY OR POWER?

130. Agree or disagree: Rich people are crazy.

131. Who's got the better set of pipes—Beyoncé or Christina Aguilera?

132. HAVE YOU EVER HAD YOUR HEART BROKEN?

133. If you had to eat from one fast-food restaurant for the rest of your life, which one would it be?

134. Which of your friends would get kicked off **SURVIVOR** first? **THE AMAZING RACE**? **AMERICAN IDOL**?

135. What would you rather have magically fit in your locker—a full-length mirror or a mini-fridge?

136. FAVORITE CHILDHOOD TOY?

137. Fun or dangerous: paintball.

138. What would you rather live in—eternal night or eternal day?

139. Waffle House or Denny's? If you don't know the restaurants, consider yourself, your arteries, and your anus lucky, and proceed to the next question.

140. AGREE OR DISAGREE: SMOKING CIGARETTES MAKES YOU LOOK COOL.

141. What is your idea of heaven? Hell?

142. Would you ever go to a nude beach? Under what circumstances?

143. If you were in a slasher/horror film, how would you prefer to die?

144. Your friend gets a speeding ticket while giving you a lift. Do you chip in to pay for the ticket?

145. IF YOU COULD OPEN A BUSINESS WITH YOUR BEST FRIENDS, WHAT WOULD IT BE?

146. Your good friend gets a tattoo, and they **REALLY** like it . . . but you notice a spelling or punctuation error. Do you pull out a red Sharpie and fix it, or do you keep your mouth shut?

147. AGREE OR DISAGREE: EVERY LAND-MASS IS ESSENTIALLY AN ISLAND.

148. Would you rather live with a boring pothead or an erratic alcoholic?

149. Would you rather be sneezed on or spit on?

150. You can't stand the person your best friend is dating and do **NOT** understand how they could put up with such a 24/7 shit-show. Do you intervene or let it be?

151. DESCRIBE YOUR PERFECT DATE.

152. If forced to, what man-eating predator would you keep as a pet?

153. Should music be free? Should movies? If you think they should be, where do you draw the line on what deserves to be paid for and what doesn't?

154. HOT OR NOT: BLACK-AND-WHITE MOVIES.

155. Your best friend—drunk as a skunk—kisses you at their birthday party. What do you do? Is it rude to not humor them on their birthday?

156. Forget the damn birthday party. Would you make out with your best friend for twenty dollars?

157. WHICH IS WORSE—HAVING YOUR PROM CLOTHES SUPERWRINKLED OR STAINED? WHAT ABOUT THE NEXT MORNING?

158. Agree or disagree: People who thank God in acceptance speeches are just kissing up.

159. Do you talk to dogs or cats like they can understand you? If so, why?

160. WOULD YOU EVER CONSIDER HAVING CHILDREN? WHY OR WHY NOT?

161. Death match: George W. Bush versus an irate book club—who goes down?

162. What's the strangest turn-on you have?

163. CLOWNS: FUNNY OR SCARY? OR SEXY?

164. Agree or disagree: The Democratic Party is for young people.

165. Johnny Cash or Elvis Presley?

166. DOGS OR CATS?

167. If your best friend became a megacelebrity, would you sell their secrets to the tabloids? If so, for what price? Would your answer change if someone you hated in high school was the one to become a celebrity?

168. WHAT SONGS CAN YOU SING BY HEART? PROVE IT!

169. Do you **really** think it should be called the "World Series"?.

170. Who is the best musician (or music group) of all time? The worst?

171. You have a crush on your best friend's significant other, and what's worse, you feel like your friend takes your crush for granted. What do you do?

172. Who lies about sex more—virgins or whores?

173. If you had a mole on your face that grew hair, would you stop plucking if you were on a month-long vacation with your parents? What about with your best friends?

174. AGREE OR DISAGREE: SEX SHOULD BE A LITTLE BIT MESSY.

175. Dark chocolate or milk chocolate?

176. WHAT'S YOUR LEAST FAVORITE FORM OF EXERCISE?

177. Would you rather live the life of a rock star or a movie star?

178. Whose career is the most over?

a. Whitney Houston

b. Backstreet Boys

c. Jessica Simpson

d. Avril Lavigne

179. What product would you most like to be the spokeswhore for?

180. LEAST FAVORITE AMERICAN IDOL?

181. Agree or disagree: Jesus was a carpenter.

182. If you were a cop, would you be the good cop or bad cop?

183. What's the worst nickname you've ever had? Is there a . . . BEST nickname someone's ever given you?

184. WHICH WOULD YOU GIVE UP FOR LIFE: SEX OR LAUGHTER?

185. Would you rather have an infestation of mice or roaches? (Big, fat roaches . . .)

186. Dungeons & Dragons or STAR WARS convention?

187. Is it better to be late or early?

188. HOT OR NOT: FUR.

189. Is it more romantic to have a song written about you or a portrait painted of you?

190. Who is sadder? People with three or more cats, or people with three or more jobs?

191. AGREE OR DISAGREE: ONCE A CHEATER, ALWAYS A CHEATER.

192. Could you date your sworn enemy's sibling?

193. Do you wish on falling stars? Why or why not?

194. WHAT INVENTION ARE YOU WAITING FOR?

195. Who do you consider to be the most attractive Disney cartoon character?

196. WHAT'S ONE DRUG YOU ABSOLUTELY WILL NOT TRY?

197. Least favorite sexual position?

198. Would you say something if you noticed your friend gaining or losing too much weight?

199. What's your biggest regret so far in life? Which of your accomplishments are you most proud of?

200. You suspect the reason your teacher is so jolly at ten A.M. is because her water bottle might be filled with . . . special water. How best to verify your claim?

201. Your cougar of a mother starts dating a second-year senior at your school. How best to tame said cougar?

202. WHAT MAGAZINE OR NEWSPAPER WOULD YOU MOST LIKE TO BE PROFILED IN?

203. What's worse on a woman—dark facial hair or hairy moles?

204. HOT OR NOT: I.H.O.P.

205. You're stuck driving behind someone going five m.p.h. under the speed limit, making full and complete stops at every stop sign, with their left blinker on . . . for miles. And you're on a single-lane, double-yellow-line road. What do you do?

206. Guy-and-girl couple: At what point does height difference (girl taller, guy shorter) become . . . weird? (If you don't think **ANY** amount of height difference is weird, then bully for you, you perfect human being, you!)

207. Agree or disagree: I could enslave my genetically identical clone.

208. BEST AGE TO HAVE A BABY? GET MARRIED? RETIRE?

209. Do you primarily use your right or your left hand to masturbate? If you **DON'T** masturbate, you should just know that you'll go blind if you don't. Kidding! But if you don't, um . . . well, when you try it, come back to this question.

210. Who would you most like to punch in the face?

211. What insect are you most afraid of?

212. Could you be happy with a nine-to-five desk job if it meant you never had to worry about money for the rest of your life?

213. FAVORITE ANIMATED MOVIE?

214. Fun or dangerous: Drinking before going to a petting zoo.

215. DESCRIBE YOUR IDEAL ORGY. PARTICIPANTS? LOCATION? ACTIVITIES?

216. Would you rather marry the love of your life and have no friends, or never marry and have friends for life?

217. Which would you rather live without—running water or electricity?

218. Agree or disagree: Janet Jackson's Super Bowl wardrobe malfunction released evil into this world, and **SHOULD HAVE** been punished as such!

219. Where were you on September 11?

220. HOT OR NOT: KNITTING.

221. Walking down a dark, deserted street alone, what are you most paranoid about happening?

222. On a scale of 1 to 10—10 being the most IN DENIAL—how stubborn are people who still think global warming is made up?

223. Your favorite DVD is missing after you've hosted a big sleepover. Do you interrogate your friends? Or do you sorta suspect one of them already?

224. Is there such a thing as too much sex? Too much masturbation?

225. IF YOU HAD TO KILL AND PREPARE YOUR OWN MEAT, WOULD YOU BECOME A VEGETARIAN?

226. You **HAVE** to pick someone over fifty years old to sleep with. Who would it be?

227. After how many dates with someone is it weird to not consider that person your girlfriend or boyfriend?

228. What's worse—having a hot mom or a hot little sister?

229. FAVORITE SYNTHETIC FABRIC?

230. Fun or dangerous: Jet Skis.

231. COULD YOU EVER TAKE A VOW OF CELIBACY?

232. What's your least favorite catchphrase?

233. Agree or disagree: I have eaten a scab.

234. DO YOU FEEL BAD FOR SUPERSTARS UNDER SIEGE BY THE PAPARAZZI?

235. Redheads or blondes?

236. Have you ever walked in on your parent(s) having sex? If so, break through your self-imposed mental blocks and describe in detail.

237. DEATH MATCH: A PIRATE WITH A REMOVABLE PEG LEG VERSUS A FLOCK OF PARROTS?

238. If you had to quit either bathing or brushing your teeth for a week, which would you choose?

239. IF YOU WERE FORCED TO HAVE A DISABILITY, WHICH WOULD YOU CHOOSE FOR YOURSELF?

240. Agree or disagree: I have something to contribute to society.

241. You find someone's lost driver's license. They're twenty-two, you're seventeen. They have brown hair and blue eyes—and **HEY**, so do you! In fact, this person could pass for a slightly older sibling. You see where this is going, right? Do you contact the owner of the driver's license, or do you keep it and head to the closest liquor store?

242. IS IT BETTER TO BE A MORNING PERSON OR A NIGHT OWL?

243. Which reality TV show would you most like to be on?

244. What's the most rolling-around-on-the-ground, clutching-your-side, laugh-till-you-cry video you've seen online?

245. WHICH MINORITY IN AMERICA HAS IT THE WORST OVERALL?

246. If you had to choose between your birth control or your acne medication, which would you choose and why?

247. Fun or dangerous: painkillers.

248. Which singer has had the most successful solo career after leaving his/her group? Which singer do you think most needs to go solo?

249. IF YOU HAD TO PICK A PLACE TO LIVE FOR THE REST OF YOUR LIFE, WHERE WOULD IT BE?

250. If you copied off of a friend's test, but it was your friend who was blamed for cheating, would you stand up and take the fall?

251. Which sport is the most homoerotic?

252. Is it better to be tactless or oblivious?

253. ARE YOU AFRAID OF DEATH?

254. Death match: A frat house versus a pack of stiletto-armed drag queens?

255. If you killed someone and had to dispose of the body, how would you do it?

256. What do you think the world would be like without religion?

257. AGREE OR DISAGREE: THERE ARE FOUR QUARTS IN A GALLON.

258. Ellen or Tyra?

259. SIX FLAGS OR SIX FLASKS?

260. If you had to pick one celebrity to dress up as, in drag, who would it be?

261. What was the worst book assigned by your English teacher? What was the best?

262. DESCRIBE YOUR IDEAL ALL-NIGHTER.

263. What's worse: a life without music, or a life without movies?

264. HOT OR NOT: CIGARS.

265. If you had to be trapped for all eternity with one celebrity, who would it be?

266. What is the most ridiculous baby name you have ever heard?

267. AGREE OR DISAGREE: IT IS SOMETIMES NECESSARY TO LIE.

268. At what point is one's virginity lost? What about girls who like girls and boys who like boys?

269. If you were given your own fashion line, what would your "look" be? Describe one piece of clothing from your fabulously fictional collection.

270. WHAT IS YOUR IDEAL VACATION?

271. Death match: **TYRANNOSAURUS REX** versus a convoy of Hummers?

272. If you didn't have to work for a living, what would you do with your time?

273. WHAT MAJOR CELEBRITY WILL DIE NEXT?

274. Agree or disagree: Oprah could be elected President of the United States.

275. Which animal would you pick to be and why?

276. Besides all that crap in November and December, what is your favorite holiday?

277. WHO WOULD WIN IN A CRACK-SMOKING CONTEST: AMY WINEHOUSE OR PETE DOHERTY?

278. Do you ever give yourself "naked time" when you're alone in the house?

279. If you were a competitive eater, what eating contest would be your forte?

280. How much is a good tip? What's the least you would tip for bad service? If you noticed a friend or family member leaving a bad tip, would you say something? If so, how?

281. HOT OR NOT: COED DORMS.

282. Under what circumstances—if any—would you have sex without a condom?

283. Would you choose to be in a coma or cryogenically frozen?

284. AGREE OR DISAGREE: CARING MEANS SHARING.

285. As long as you were unaware of it, would you rather have someone spit in your soup or your salad?

286. Your best friend shares their really bad novel with you. (Note: Feel free to swap "novel" with anything arts related—contrived modern-dance piece, melted-Solo-cup sculpture, a train wreck of an overpriced play, whatever!) Do you blow some nice hot air up their ass? Or do you share your true feelings?

287. Who's the most evil person alive today? The most good?

288. What song would you rather have stuck in your head all day long—"When the Saints Go Marching In" or "Lady Marmalade"?

289. WHAT IS THE LEAST SEXY PART OF THE BODY?

290. Favorite serial killer?

291. Agree or disagree: Madonna is a robot.

292. Would you rather spend your day at a rodeo or a grand prix racetrack?

293. WOULD YOU RATHER GIVE UP YOUR CELL PHONE OR YOUR COMPUTER?

294. What do you consider to be "your porn"? Trashy romances? ESPN? **PORN?**

295. Would you rather have a gay dad or a gay mom?

296. If you got to have a steamy night of passion with someone from any country in the world (other than your own, Pollyanna), which would it be?

297. HOT OR NOT: SCARS.

298. Would you rather live with the Addams Family or the Munsters?

299. Would you rather have a burping problem or a sweating problem?

300. Agree or disagree: Farting is grosser than picking your nose.

301. WHAT IS THE WORST COMMON LIE?

302. Life-and-death situation! A kid from school and one of their parents both need it, and they need it **BAD**: mouth to mouth. Who gets saved by your wind-tunnel CPR kisses?

303. WOULD YOU RATHER LIVE WITH PYGMIES OR ESKIMOS?

304. Would you solicit a friend to help examine you for evidence of an STD . . . down there?

305. What's more embarrassing—a dad in sandals and socks, or a dad in short shorts? A mom in a Juicy Couture sweatsuit or a mom in a Kmart sweatsuit?

306. WHAT'S YOUR FAVORITE PARTY GAME?

(Thiiiis one?)

307. Agree or disagree: Anorexia is sometimes necessary.

308. When you're elderly, would you rather have to use a walker or a scooter?

309. WHAT WOULD BE YOUR IDEAL TATTOO?

310. Are you for or against Internet porn on the family computer?

311. What's the grossest thing you'd ever eat? Would you eat dog? Insects? Bull testicles? What's the grossest thing you **HAVE** eaten?

312. Would you try coke if you had a sober and trustworthy friend watching out for you? Would your answer change if the drug in question did?

313. HOT OR NOT: JOHN STAMOS.

314. Is it okay to steal cable service?

315. Which of the United States is the least necessary?

316. Agree or disagree: I might have seen a ghost.

317. CAKE OR PIE?

318. If a machete-wielding psycho were all of a sudden ten feet away from you, what would your escape route be?

319. Okay, totally gross, but you HAVE to pick one animal on Planet Earth to have sex with. What would it be?

320. WOULD YOU PAY A HOBO TO BUY YOU BOOZE?

321. If there were suddenly a musical based on your most recent life crisis, what would it be called?

322. Favorite condiment?

323. Fun or dangerous: Throwing shit off a bridge.

324. WHAT DO YOU THINK PEOPLE LIKE THE LEAST ABOUT YOU?

325. Is learning about history important? Why or why not?

326. Agree or disagree: It is sometimes okay to steal from friends.

327. Do you want to be remembered? If so, how?

328. WHAT WOULD YOU RATHER SNORT—SUGAR, FLOUR, OR SALT?

329. How important is it for someone to get the birds-and-the-bees talk from a family member rather than in school? Do you think sex education is important?

330. Death match: Dick Cheney versus the Ghosts of Christmas Past, Present, and Future. What if we throw Tiny Tim in the mix?

331. Do you think a viable cure for AIDS will be available in your lifetime?

332. What would be the most badass hybrid animal you can imagine? (And you can't say "liger" if you've seen **NAPOLEON DYNAMITE**.)

333. AGREE OR DISAGREE: MACHINES WILL ONE DAY TAKE OVER EARTH.

334. Is it worse to forget someone's face or someone's name?

335. IF YOU COULD REMEMBER BEING BORN, WOULD YOU WANT TO?

336. Would you ever skinny-dip with members of the opposite sex (or, if you swing that way, members of the same sex)? In the daylight?

337. Which would you rather have be public knowledge—your recorded phone conversations or Internet usage?

338. If you were camping, and you were afraid of wolves, bears, or something equally nature-related and frightening, would you drop a deuce ten feet away from your best friend if they were keeping lookout?

339. Your grandmother has been sick for months and says she is ready to die. Could you pull the plug?

340. FUN OR DANGEROUS: INTERNATIONAL FIELD TRIPS.

341. Should people older than thirty be on Facebook?

342. Describe your ideal road trip. Where would you go? Who would you bring? Who would you **MEET**?

343. Agree or disagree: People who read newspapers are smarter.

344. IN A CRISIS SITUATION, WOULD YOU BE A LEADER OR A FOLLOWER?

345. Would you rather be a maid or a garbage man?

346. If you had a choice of how you'd kick the bucket, what would it be?

347. DEATH MATCH: THE OLSEN TWINS VERSUS PEREZ HILTON.

348. Who would be most horrified to hear your answers to this book's questions?

349. How do you explain your actions to Larry King? What do you do if he dies mid-sentence?

350. Agree or disagree: The homeless are dangerous.

351. Your band takes off in your senior year of high school. Do you try to finish school on the road or go AWOL for a year? Or just drop out?

352. WHO WOULD WIN IN A FIGHT: TYRA OR TYRA'S EGO?

353. What's your "dream class" that isn't offered at your school? **If** you don't have one, make one up!

354. Sex in a hot tub or sex in the ocean?

355. WILL THE HUMAN RACE EVER GO EXTINCT?

356. It's the last day of high school, and the hottest teacher who you've been crushing on since day one of freshman year asks if you want to get a coffee. Innocent enough, right? And you're eighteen—you can do what you want now! Do you say yes?

357. Hot or not: oysters on the half shell.

358. WHAT'S WORSE—TOO MUCH MAKEUP OR TOO MUCH PERFUME?

359. Which is grosser—beige or electric blue?

360. AGREE OR DISAGREE: THE BOOK IS ALWAYS BETTER THAN THE MOVIE.

361. What do you say to your creepy aunt or uncle who won't stop flirting with your teenage friends?

362. If you were given $100,000 to spend in a month, how would you spend it? (Note that spending in this case is **NOT** the same as investing. You gotta get rid of it all, baby, so have at it!)

363. What would you do if you knew one of your parents was cheating on the other one?

364. Death match: Mufasa versus the hunter who killed Bambi's mother.

365. WOULD YOU KILL A KITTEN FOR WORLD PEACE?

366. Could you eat human flesh if you had to?

367. Agree or disagree: Those who can't do, teach.

368. Do you consider yourself voyeuristic? What's the most voyeuristic thing you've ever done?

369. PENTHOUSE OR MANSION? OR NEITHER?

370. Who would you rather meet in a dark alley: Amy Winehouse or Britney Spears? And . . . WHY?

371. Who would win in a drinking contest: Amy Winehouse or Britney Spears?

372. WOULD YOU RATHER BE TALENTED OR SUCCESSFUL?

373. If you could live without either sleeping or eating, which would you pick?

374. If you have one, describe your dream wedding in detail. If you don't have one, be a sport and make one up, for chrissakes!

375. HOT OR NOT: CEMETERY SEX.

376. Pepsi or Coke?

377. Do you like school, and if not, what would make you like school? Okay, now how about **IN REALITY**, what could be **DONE** to make you like school more?

378. AGREE OR DISAGREE: BACKWOODS IS BACK IN STYLE.

379. Peanut butter—crunchy or smooth?

380. WHAT'S THE MOST FUCKED-UP DREAM YOU'VE EVER HAD?

381. What book **HAS** to be made into a movie?

382. Your friend is on antidepressants, and you think they're making them act strange. It's starting to worry you—what do you do?

383. What gives you the best perks: a friend who's a waiter or a friend who works at the movies?

384. You're out with your best friend, and while you've been a totally responsible sober sister, your friend has been drinking . . . and when it's time to head home, he or she refuses to hand over the keys and let you drive. What do you do? What if your friend gets all pissed and threatens to abandon you in the parking lot?

385. AGREE OR DISAGREE: I AM ATTRACTED TO STUFFED ANIMALS.

386. What's the most annoying way to say good-bye to someone?

387. Which would you rather possess, and why: the power of invisibility or the ability to fly?

388. Your friends want you to help them shoplift, but only as a lookout. Do you?

389. WHAT'S THE FUNNIEST ROMANTIC COMEDY? THE MOST ROMANTIC? THE MOST ANNOYING?

390. Debate team or chess club?

391. Do you think abstinence-only sex education works?

392. HOT OR NOT: SEX TOYS.

393. Would you tell someone if they were a mean drunk? What if it's your best friend?

394. You just found out you're adopted. Will you search for your birth parents?

395. AGREE OR DISAGREE: MANNERS ARE IMPORTANT.

396. Would you rather see a public protest or public art?

397. If you had to ride either a go-cart or a Segway for life, which would you choose?

398. IN WHAT TIME AND PLACE IN HISTORY (OTHER THAN THE PRESENT) WOULD YOU MOST LIKE TO LIVE?

399. When you die, what do you want done with the remains? Burial? Cremation? Burial at sea?

400. FAMILY GUY or THE SIMPSONS?

401. Sexiest historical figure? Come on, you know you love Millard Fillmore. . . .

402. Agree or disagree: Gay people are more fun.

403. Where are you most ticklish?

404. WOULD YOU RATHER BE ATTACKED BY A BEAR OR A SHARK?

405. Your boy- or girlfriend surprises you in bed one day by taking a naked picture of you. Your reaction: "Delete that!" or "Now it's your turn!"

406. Who makes the best ice cream?

407. Which movie do you most want to see remade?

408. YOU FIND A WAD OF CASH IN THE LIBRARY. DO YOU KEEP IT OR TRY TO FIND THE PERSON IT BELONGS TO?

409. Would you rather be independently wealthy, or wealthy because of your family?

410. What do you do if your mom or dad is growing a painfully visible cold sore and appears not to notice or care?

411. Agree or disagree: I am attracted to myself.

412. Is it worse to have something green stuck in your teeth or something green poking out of your nose?

413. DO YOU HAVE RECURRING DREAMS? IF SO, DESCRIBE ONE.

414. Which sport would be the best to play naked?

415. Which is worse—a music snob or a movie snob?

416. HOW YOUNG IS TOO YOUNG?

417. Favorite vulgar expression?

418. Fun or dangerous: Ouija board.

419. Which is worse, a know-nothing or a know-it-all?

420. What's the biggest deal-breaker when it comes to a person you're dating?

421. AGREE OR DISAGREE: MARRIAGE IS A CIVIL RIGHT.

422. Would you rather be stalked by a complete stranger or your best friend?

423. What is the maximum number of people you would have sex with at the same time?

424. DEATH MATCH: CELINE DION VERSUS DOLLY PARTON.

425. Do you ever make New Year's resolutions, and if so, do you ever keep them?

426. Did you know that if you bite down hard on a Wint O Green Life Saver in the dark, it makes a spark? Try it!

427. Agree or disagree: I drink too much.

428. GUYS, WHAT'S THE BEST WAY TO HIDE A CLASSROOM ERECTION? GIRLS, DOES IT WORK?

429. Your books are shut, and Google has crashed. Can you name two countries that border Iraq? Whoever does it first wins . . . **RESPECT!**

430. World peace or eternal personal financial security?

431. Chips and dip, or chips and salsa?

432. Would you be supportive if your newly single parent wanted cosmetic surgery?

433. FAVORITE MOVIE SEX SCENE?

434. You hear a mean joke about your best friend. Do you tell him or her? What if you feel like it would help to tell, even if it might hurt your friend's feelings?

435. Who is the most overrated singer alive today?

436. You're flying transatlantic with your significant other. The entire plane is asleep, somewhere between Newfoundland and Iceland. Do you dare join the Mile High Club? What about getting a little friendly under the scratchy airline-provided blanket?

437. AGREE OR DISAGREE: LIP-SYNCHING IS A COP-OUT.

438. Would you give up your favorite food for LIFE for washboard abs?

439. Krispy Kreme or Dunkin' Donuts?

440. WHAT MOVIE GENRE BEST DESCRIBES YOUR REAL LIFE?

441. Death match: The cast of **HIGH SCHOOL MUSICAL 3** versus the monsters from **SESAME STREET**.

442. Old-school animation cartoons or computer-animation cartoons?

443. Getting locked out of your house, or inside your house . . . which is scarier?

444. AGREE OR DISAGREE: ALL MEN ARE CREATED EQUAL.

445. What would be the most hilarious cover for a surprise party?

446. A hot car or the power to teleport?

447. Skydiving or bungee jumping?

448. WHICH IS HARDER WORK—MOWING LAWNS OR CLEANING POOLS?

449. SEX IN PUBLIC PLACES! Where's the easiest place to do the nasty outside the comfort of your own home (or car)?

450. Canadians? A little weird . . . or just like you and me?

451. FUN OR DANGEROUS: RIDING YOUR BIKE DOWN A SLIDE.

452. Would you rather be a stereotypically beautiful class-A moron or a Nobel Prize winner with a gimp arm?

453. KARAOKE BY FORCE! Pick your top five songs.

454. AGREE OR DISAGREE: THE GOVERNMENT IS COVERING UP THE EXISTENCE OF ALIENS.

455. IS IT BETTER TO BE THE OLDEST, MIDDLE, OR YOUNGEST SIBLING?

456. What is the most you could imagine giving to a charity, and what charity would it be? If you had to, what cause would you give everything you owned to?

457. What's the worst holiday to spend alone?

458. DEATH MATCH: YOU VERSUS SPIDER MONKEYS WIELDING BUTTER KNIVES.

459. What's scarier to discuss: politics or poetry?

460. WHAT'S WORSE: CHILD LABOR OR ELDERLY LABOR?

461. You have a hickey in a fairly obvious place. Cover up or wear with pride?

462. The Beatles or the Rolling Stones?

463. You've been DYING to get a piercing in a pretty . . . intimate place. Sadly, you're not of age, and your parents would ground you to Earth's fiery core if they knew, let alone consented. But your cool older sister knows a guy who could do it on the DL . . . her **BOYFRIEND**! Are you down with getting that up-close and personal with your possible future brother-in-law?

464. You have food poisoning. To put it as delicately as possible . . . which end would you rather have "it" coming out of three or four times an hour?

465. WHICH REALITY TV SHOW IS THE MOST SCRIPTED?

466. Harelip or hair loss?

467. What's the best music to have sex to? Smoke pot to? Dance to? Drive to?

468. HOT OR NOT: THE MAFIA.

469. Who would you rather have sex with—Rosie O'Donnell or Donald Trump?

470. Seriously, though . . . what is the **WORST** thing that's ever happened to you?

471. Agree or disagree: The Internet will one day replace the need for knowledge.

472. SCHOOL LUNCH OR BAG LUNCH?

473. What is the worst thing about babies?

474. Have you ever seriously contemplated suicide? Even just for a second?

475. Which accent do you think best goes with the following animals?

a. Cat

b. Hamster

c. Goldfish

d. Iguana

476. WHAT'S SOMETHING THAT SETS YOU APART FROM EVERYONE ELSE?

477. Which **PROJECT RUNWAY** designer would you want to design what you wear to your wedding?

478. Agree or disagree: **I have friends I would not invite to a party.**

479. Does size **REALLY** matter? How big is too big? (And how small is too small?)

480. If you were bullied (or are still being bullied), what's the worst bullying you've ever been the target of? If you **ARE** a bully, what's the worst (or best?) bullying you've ever done?

481. Okay, weird one, but you have to choose a household object to have sex with. (Keep your seats, people, this isn't a dare!) What would you pick?

482. WOULD YOU RATHER FREEZE TO DEATH OR BURN TO DEATH?

482. Boxers or briefs? Or boxer briefs? It's a totally stupid question, so, to make it interesting, explain your reasoning.

484. HOT OR NOT: VEGETARIANS.

485. Would you rather be hot and popular in high school or in your early twenties?

486. If you were to have a sex-change operation, which would you have done first: uptown or downtown?

487. What's more important—friendship or gas money?

488. WHAT IS THE LAST PART OF YOUR BODY YOU'D HAVE WAXED?

489. If you had to be any celebrity's personal assistant (read: slave), who would it be?

490. If you could pick one friend to be **YOUR** personal assistant, who would it be?

491. Is world peace possible? Does it matter?

492. WHAT IS THE WEIRDEST BREED OF DOG?

493. What's the longest you've gone without changing your underwear?

494. What is your favorite stereotype?

495. Agree or disagree: Single people are more fun.

---

496. Who deserves his or her own talk show? Which current talk-show host doesn't deserve it?

497. WHAT'S YOUR STANCE ON GUN CONTROL?

498. What would you do if you saw someone keying a car in your school parking lot?

499. What would the name for your celebrity perfume or cologne be?

500. If you could learn any language, what would it be?

ABOUT THE AUTHORS

NICO MEDINA is the author of **The Straight Road to Kylie** and **Fat Hoochie Prom Queen** (Simon Pulse, 2007 and 2008). He vowed to never go to school again after receiving his BA in sociology from the University of Florida, and is now a managing editor at a publishing house in New York City. Nico **would** kill a kitten for world peace, but he wouldn't like it.

BILLY MERRELL is the author of **Talking in the Dark**, a poetry memoir (Scholastic, 2003), and co-editor of **The Full Spectrum: A New Generation of Writing about GLBT and Other Identities** (Knopf, 2006), which received a 2006 Lambda Literary Award. He spends his days doing web development for Poets.org. If

Billy had to kill and prepare his own meat, he **would** become a vegetarian . . . though he might still eat fish.

NICO AND BILLY met in 2001 while studying at the University of Florida. They forged a relationship based on honesty and fast food in 2002, moved to New York in 2004, and married in 2008. They now live in Brooklyn, with their pug-daughter, Paisley (who thinks Taco Bell is hot). Visit them online at www.nicoandbilly.com.

DON'T JOIN THE PARTY. BE THE PARTY.

★★★★★★★★★★★★★★★★★

from Simon Pulse
PUBLISHED BY SIMON & SCHUSTER